The Old Witch
and
The Ghost Parade

by Ida DeLage

illustrated by Jody Taylor

GARRARD PUBLISHING COMPANY
CHAMPAIGN, ILLINOIS

Copyright © 1978 by Ida DeLage
All rights reserved. Manufactured in the U.S.A.
International Standard Book Number: 0-8116-4062-0
Library of Congress Catalog Card Number: 77-17185

The Old Witch
and
The Ghost Parade

The old witch of the hill
woke up.
She rubbed her eyes.
"Ho hum," she said.
"What shall I do today?"
Then, all of a sudden,
she remembered.
It was Halloween!
The old witch jumped
out of bed fast.

"I have to hurry,"
said the witch.
"I need lots and lots
of magic brew for Halloween.
I have to cast
a lot of spells today.
Hee-hee-hee!"

6

The old witch stirred her pot.

She put in
    6 rotten eggs
    5 wiggle worms
    4 slimy snails
    3 hairy spiders
    2 creepy bugs
    1 blue boogle beetle
    lots and lots of toadstools
    and a big jug
    of smelly swamp water.

"I hope this brew
isn't too magic,"
said the witch.

The old witch
put some brew
into her jug.
Then she hopped
on her broom.
"I will go and see,"
she said,
"if the little kids
are getting ready
for trick or treat."

The witch flew down the hill
and over the valley.
"Oh ho!" she said.
"Something is going on
at the town hall.
I wonder what it is."

The old witch swooped down
and hid behind a tree.
She saw the mayor put a sign
on the town hall door.

"A ghost parade!"
said the witch.
"Oh what fun!
I can be a ghost.
I will be in the parade.
I love prizes."

"I'll get a big pumpkin,"
said the witch.
"I will make the biggest
jack-o'-lantern in the world."
But when the old witch went
to her pumpkin patch,
what did she see?

"My pumpkins are too small,"
said the witch.
"But I know what to do."
The witch put some magic brew
all over the little pumpkins.
She said,
"Little pumpkins in a row,
grow and grow and GROW."

The little pumpkins
began to grow.
They got bigger and BIGGER.
All of a sudden,
there was a BOOM!

Pumpkin seeds flew
all over the old witch.
"I knew it!" cried the witch.
"My brew was too magic.
I shouldn't have put in
that blue boogle beetle."

The old witch shook her broom.
"Stop!" she cried.

"Big fat pumpkins in a row,

do not grow.

Do not grow."

The pumpkins stopped growing.

The old witch took

the biggest, fattest pumpkin.

She flew back to her cave.
"Now," said the witch.
"I will make
the scariest jack-o'-lantern
in the whole world.
Hee-hee-hee!"

Just then,
some children were running
through the woods.
They stopped to pick
some wild flowers.
"Hey!" called Jerry.
"See what I found.
Pumpkins in the woods!
They must be wild pumpkins."
"Hurray!" said Polly.
"Just what we need
to make jack-o'-lanterns."
The children looked at
all the pumpkins.
"I'll take a big, round one,"
said Molly.

"Now we can be
in the ghost parade,"
said Jack.

At that very moment,
the old witch of the hill
peeked out of her cave.
She saw the children
in her pumpkin patch.

The witch ran down the hill.
She shook her broom.
"Ee-eek!" screeched the witch.
She hopped up and down.
"Get out of here!" she yelled.

"Run!" yelled Jack.
"It's the old witch."
The children ran down the hill.
Molly dropped her pumpkin.
It got to the bottom of the hill
before she did.

24

"The old witch
doesn't like anyone to go
near her cave," said Molly.
"Let's go to my house
and make our jack-o'-lanterns."
"Gee!" said Jack.
"My pumpkin is getting heavy."
Then—all of a sudden—

Jack's pumpkin
turned into a rock.
Molly's pumpkin
melted into a puddle.
Jerry's pumpkin
flew up into the apple tree.
Polly's pumpkin
turned into a jelly bean.

The old witch swished by
on her broom.
She laughed, "Hee-hee-hee!"
"Oh!" said the children.

"Those pumpkins were magic.
They must have been
the old witch's pumpkins.
And she's very angry."

The children ran
down the road.
"Look!" said Jerry.
"See the big pile of pumpkins."
"I hope they are not magic,"
said Molly.
"These pumpkins are 25¢,"
said the farmer.
"Oh!" said the children.
"We don't have any money."
"Boo-hoo-hoo!" cried Polly.
"We have no pumpkins
to make jack-o'-lanterns.
We can't be in
the ghost parade."
The old farmer felt sorry.

"By gollys," he said.
"Every little kid should have
a jack-o'-lantern on Halloween."
The farmer made a sign.
He put it by
some little pumpkins.

"Oh goody!" cried the children.

"Free pumpkins.

We like little pumpkins

the best anyway.

Thank you, Mr. Farmer."

The children ran home

to make their jack-o'-lanterns.

It was seven o'clock.
A lot of ghosts were coming
to the ghost parade.

The ghosts had jack-o'-lanterns.
Some had happy faces.
Some had scary faces.

The mayor stood
on the town hall steps.
"The ghost parade
will now start," he said.
"The parade will go
around the town clock
and back again."

"And now,"
said the mayor,
"I will pick
the best jack-o'-lanterns.
Hold your jack-o'-lanterns
up high
so I can see them all."

"Well," said the mayor.
"There are so
many good ones,
it's hard to pick
the best jack-o'-lanterns."
All of a sudden,
a ghost came up.
The ghost had a BROOM!
And it had
a great, big,
scary jack-o'-lantern.
"Oh!" everyone said.
"Look at that scary face.
The mayor will pick
that scary jack-o'-lantern
for the first prize."

The mayor looked and looked.
At last he said,
"Smiles are always
better than frowns.
I give the first prize to—
four little ghosts."

"The first prize," said the mayor,

"is a HAYRIDE

all around the town."

"Hurray!"

yelled the four little ghosts.

"And now," said the mayor.
"I will give the second prize.
It is this scary GHOST BOOK.
It will make your hair
stand up straight.
Ha-ha-ha!"

Suddenly,
all the jack-o'-lantern lights
went out.

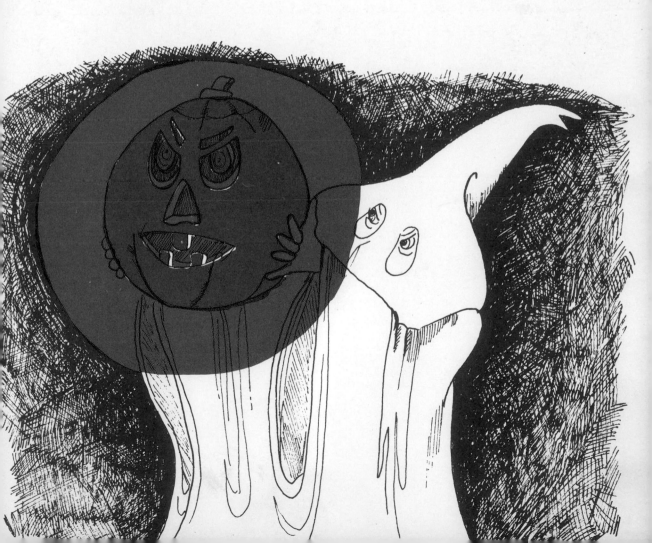

The scary jack-o'-lantern went
"Ooo-oo-oo!"
Smoke came out of its nose.
Sparks flew out of its ears.
"Wow!" said the mayor.
"That's the scariest
jack-o'-lantern in the world!"

Suddenly,
there was a big flash
and a BOOM!
A skinny hand
snatched the GHOST BOOK
right out of the mayor's hand!

A ghost zipped off on a broom.
The scary jack-o'-lantern
glowed in the sky.
"What happened?" everyone asked.
The four little ghosts knew,
but they wouldn't tell.

They hid in the hay
until that scary jack-o'-lantern
went far, far away.

Her cat is by the fire.
Her pumpkin's on the shelf.
The witch reads the GHOST BOOK
and scares herself!

Aa ad